Islands

The 2023 Capricorn Coast Writers Festival

Student Writers Anthology

First published in 2023 by the Capricorn Coast Writers Festival
Website: www.capricorncoastwritersfestival.com

Copyright © Capricorn Coast Writers Festival

Cover design by Elaine Ouston

ISBN 9780648737667 (paperback)

A catalogue record for this book is available from the National Library of Australia

Table of contents

Primary (Years 4 - 6) category

Secondary (Years 7 – 10) category

Secondary (Years 11 and12) category

Yeppoon Rotary Introduction

Congratulations to the budding authors who have had their short stories published in this Anthology.

Yeppoon Rotary is excited to again be involved in the Student Short Story Competition, a key initiative of the Capricorn Coast Writers Festival. The Rotary club has a long history of working with and supporting students across the Capricorn Coast. With one of the core priorities of Rotary being education, we were pleased to be asked to be a sponsor.

The collection of stories in this Anthology celebrates the excellence in creative writing, showcasing the local talent in the Capricorn Coast. May these students become our Authors of the future.

Peta Bosomworth
President
Yeppoon Rotary Club

Festival Foreword

Now in its second year, the Capricorn Coast Writers Festival Student Short Story Competition was once again a fantastic component of a packed programme of events.

The theme and title of the competition, 'Islands,' ignited a hugely enthusiastic response from students and teachers alike. With the title meaning so many different things to students of all ages, the range of entries was quite astonishing and proved how fortunate we are to have such passionate young storytellers living here on the coast.

The competition judges agreed that with the standard of entries so high, it was a tough job to pick the winners and I'd like to thank them very much for taking such a thorough and considered approach. The presentation of prizes took place at Yeppoon Town Hall on the first full day of the festival, where an electric atmosphere heralded an explosion of excited applause as each winning entry was announced. A truly memorable occasion!

My sincere thanks to Rotary Club of Yeppoon for supporting this initiative and thank you to everyone who wrote a story. They are an absolute joy to read—please enjoy!

Nene Davies
Festival Founder

Anguished Seed

A poem by Olive Allen

Sacred Heart Catholic Primary School

The big grey van crosses the horizon making the red, yellow
and orange light bounce off the windows.
A seed suddenly pops into my trembling hand.
When it makes contact a dagger stabs me in the heart.
I throw it out the window,
It is buried in the sand
Unknown land.
The days slowly trickle by like the sand in an hourglass.
The sand is an unseen colour,
Before now
Black. Red. Blue.
Every night something uncontrollable fills my bones, my heart,
my soul
The green leaves turn brown. The blue sky turns black. The co-
lourful flowers - disintegrate.
Silence.
My feelings are bottled up inside me and I feel like I am about to
explode!
KABOOM!

Islands

The sand blows about making a horrific hurricane but not just that,
The children cry. The adults scream. The dog's howl rattles the windows. But also the mind and the soul.
Silence
Sadness
Stillness
The world is gone
The universe in gone
Everything in gone.
Except for sand, rubble and. And …
The seed.
The cold anguished seed
The seed of such grief and unendurable pain it could end the world and everyone in it …
But also rebuild it.
Mother nature have mercy. Mother nature have mercy …
KABOOM!
Another explosion. But this time…
The world is rebuilt
The seed is still there but that is OK.
Sadness may have ended the world but it also rebuilt it.

Note: *Olive's confident recital of her original poem at the 2023 festival, during the open mic event hosted by performance poet Joel McKerrow, earned her a place in the anthology. It is a reminder to keep-on writing and reading. The show is ongoing.*

Primary (Years 1-3)

Category

Island

By Eli M.

I was stranded on an island. This island was not a normal island. This island was ginormous. I wanted to go home but I was too sleepy, so I went to sleep.

The next day I was up and ready to build a raft and get food for the trip. I had to make an axe to get wood to build the raft.

Today, I was too tired, so I ventured to a new area of the island. I found a new animal. It was a snake. It nearly bit me on the leg, so I ran away. I was out of energy. I walked back to camp and lit a fire and caught a fish. I descaled the fish and put the fish on the fire and waited for the fish to cook. I ate the fish and went to sleep.

The next day, I started to work on the raft again. It was only half completed, so I went to sleep.

The next day, I worked really hard on the raft and finished it. I was really sleepy, so I went to sleep.

The next day, I paddled home.

Naughty James

By Emmett B.

A long time ago there was a naughty teenager called James. He had blue eyes and a massive mullet. One day, he and his family decided to go to a big island for a fishing adventure. They were extremely excited.

The family arrived on the island. Suddenly, the boat's motor broke down. They were in the middle of shark-infested waters with nowhere to go. So they went to look around the island for food and shelter but there were only trees, sand, air and grass. Luckily, in the material box they had an axe to chop down trees. So James started to chop down trees. When he was finished, the family built a raft and a paddle.

After they left, they had to work together to paddle all the way to the mainland. They were so relieved.

The Keppel Beast

By Jesse G.

It was the morning of our family fun day. We were headed to Great Keppel Island.

'Hurry up,' Mummy cried.

So we got ready and went to the harbour. We jumped in the ferry and off we went to face the island.

'Weeeeeeeeeeeeeeeeee,' Jax said as the ferry bumped up and down.

'Look,' said Tomy.

'What?' said Jax, wondering what he was looking at.

'I thought I saw something in the water.'

'Maybe it was a crocodile?'

'We're nearly there,' Lily said, looking over at the island.

'How do you know?' said Tommy.

'I'm looking at the island!' said Lily.

HONK! HONK! went the ferry.

'We're here!' said Tommy.

They all hopped off the boat.

'Lets go for a swim,' cheered Tomy.

Lily wanted a kayak.

When Lily was in the Kayak she saw the crocodile looking thing. It was definitely not a croc. It had purple spikes, sharp horns and long jaws. It was the KEPPEL BEAST!

Lily paddled back to shore and told everyone.

Even though our fun day wasn't finished, we had to go home.

The BEAST was under our ferry! But he couldn't see us.

He is now known as the KEPPEL BEAST of GKI.

Deserted Island

By Levi H.

Once there was a boat and there was a mysterious man who lived on it. No one really knew anything about him. Then one night he forgot to put his anchor down and that night he floated deep into the sea.

He woke up in the morning on a deserted island and the scary part was it was a talking island! Its name was Jeremy and he was thousands of years old.

It was a mysterious island and, Jeremy, the island, would move every night. The man was curious. He woke one night and discovered that it was an enormous turtle. It was moving around many islands. All of the islands were talking. He was in another dimension. It was pretty cool. Some of his other boat friends were there. They built a cool underwater city. They had special powers and other cool stuff in the back of all the islands. There was a giant island with special guys protecting a gem.

That would end the special dimension because it turns out he did not like the special dimension. He tried to get the gem but he didn't because he liked it.

Island Friend

By Phelicia P.

Once upon a time there was a female puppy called Millie. She had hazel blue eyes and pastel rainbow fur. Then one rainy day something bad happened to her. The city called Fisher Time Bay had a flood while she was sleeping. The flood went in her house. There was so much water it covered the roof. It swept her out to sea and when she woke up she had blurry vision from the salty water, but she could faintly see she was on a stranded island.

Millie saw a coconut and called it Jerry. Then Jerry started talking and walking. He was alive and Millie was shocked and excited at the same time. She had just made her first friend ever.

Jerry started looking at her with the biggest smile she had ever seen. He said, 'Why did the kid bring a ladder to school? Because he wanted to go to high school.' He started laughing and Millie laughed with him.

Then a woman came in a boat and said, 'Come on, Millie, it's time to go home'

Millie looked at Jerry and said, 'Got to go,

sorry. Do you want to come?'
    Jerry replied, 'Sure I'll come, thanks.'

The Waves of the Island

By Lucy Hock

Once there was a girl called November and she dreamed of going to a tropical island. She lived in the country with her dad and was far away from the ocean. Little did she know that her mother was a mermaid goddess who kept it a secret from everybody. She died when November was a baby and she had left her a magical shell that could turn her into a mermaid. November carried it in her pocket every day and never knew.

When she turned 19, she travelled to the ocean and caught her first boat to go to the closest island. It was stormy that night and, sadly, the boat sank.

She went down deep into the ocean and the sea creatures got the magic shell from her pocket and turned her into a beautiful mermaid. She could now swim in the waves of the island like her mother.

Primary (Years 4-6)

Category

Stranded on this Ancient Land

By Brianna G.

As the ferry approached the island ahead, Alison tuned out the sounds of the surrounding people and pictured a magical holiday in front of her. BASH! Water rose beneath her feet. Screams echoed around her as she jumped overboard. She was struggling to breathe in the unforgiving sea. When Alison was trying to break the surface she heard her name being called.

'ALISON!'

She blacked out.

Half opening her eyes, her vision was a blur of colours and sounds. She lay on the beach next to wavy palm trees and wondered, *where am I and who is calling my name?*

Regaining focus, she stood up searching for any signs of life on the island. After searching for many hours, Alison realised that she was the only one there. As the sun slowly went down she found shelter under a tree and crashed there for the night.

The following morning Alison hiked up the mountain, sweating from the temperature rising with each step she took. When she reached the peak of the mountain, she saw this massive crater with little splatters of steam coming out. Alison investigated it some more and knew she had to get off this island fast! As Alison sprinted down to the beach she could feel the ground slightly shaking. She could hear helicopters roaming around, so she shaped an SOS in the sand. Waving her hands everywhere, she tried to get their attention. Alison appeared to lose hope when a helicopter flew above her.

Someone called out on the loudspeaker, 'We are here to rescue you. Please remain calm.'

Alison was so relieved that she couldn't say a word. The coast guards flung down a rope and Alison started climbing. When she got to the top she happily said, 'Thanks.'

The Lava Escape

By Georgie R.

'AAAAAAAAHHHHHHHH!' screamed Holly in pure fear. She could feel her heart thudding in her chest. She could hear the sirens echoing over the small village. She jumped out of bed and threw all of her filthy clothes on. She knew what that siren meant.

Holly bolted down to the shore and could not help but gaze at the glorious and dazzling sunrise, which was slowly being hidden behind a cloud of grey ash. The locals were all scurrying down a steep hill, keeping each other closer than two peas in a pod. They were running for safety at the edge of the island, on the sand.

People were trembling. People were wailing. People were screaming in horror. They turned and saw hot, steaming lava pouring through their streets and homes, absolutely demolishing everything they owned. They had no choice but to turn to the eight small wooden kayaks.

Holly instructed while pointing to the panicked villagers, '1,2,3,4,5, you're in that boat. 1,2,3,4,5,6, head to that one!'

Finally, they were all gathered up and cramped into the kayaks, huffing and puffing. Questioning what was ahead of them, they began to paddle into the deep, dark ocean.

Following the light, which was starting to peek over the

horizon, they had a glimpse of hope. Behind them was an ocean of red lava melting, seeming to cool down. Rowing into the unknown waters, which were swarming with deadly animals was terrifying but the nearest island was a quick trip. It was known as the island of safety and that's exactly what they all needed.

Soon they could no longer see the village and all of their memories that had been crushed. On the trip, there were rumours shared about the sharks. All of a sudden, a big hungry shark rose to the surface of the water in front of Holly's kayak.

Oh no, she though to herself. She shrieked, 'Paddle as fast as you can!'

They zoomed off. Then the picturesque island appeared. Once they hit sand, all of their jaws dropped because the island was like a colour explosion!

Tired and exhausted the villagers collapsed onto the sand.

The Island of Wonder

Mahli G.

In Australia, not too long ago, there was a ten-year-old girl. Her name was Journey. Journey had an older brother named Lake. Lake was 14 years old. The siblings called themselves, the explorers, because they loved exploring rocks, forests, gardens—pretty much everything! They absolutely loved exploring.

One day, their dad, Tom, said, 'Lets go fishing on our new boat.'

'It does look like a good day for fishing,' agreed Amy, their mum, grabbing the rods from the garage.

They hooked up their boat and headed to the boat ramp. Soon after, they were sailing the sea. Soon, they stumbled across a small island. It looked like nobody had even been there.

'It's so mysterious,' said Journey, excitedly.

'It is,' replied Lake.

'Is that a sign over there?' asked Journey, unsure whether it was or not.

'It is a sign,' exclaimed Lake, looking over at the clearing. 'It says, The Island of Wonder.'

'Lets go over and have a look, shall we?'

'Definitely!'

Tom anchored their small boat and they headed to shore.

'The sand is so squishy-squashy,' said Journey, happily.

'Indeed,' said Amy.

They walked through the squishy-squashy sand. They came to a forest with terrific trees, beautiful bushes, stunning streams, lovely lakes and wicked waterfalls. It was a wonderful place!

'This must be why it is called the Island of Wonder,' said Lake.

'I wonder why we never noticed it before,' said Amy, surprised.

'I don't want to go fishing anymore, dad. I want to explore this island,' said Journey.

'You can, but don't go too far,' replied Tom.

Journey and Lake set off for their adventure. As they walked towards the beach, they felt the warm sun shining upon them.

'Look,' said Lake.

'Ooo yeah. It's sooo shiny!' replied Journey.

'Lets go and have a look.'

They walked over to the shiny object. It was a diamond! They couldn't believe their eyes! They picked it up. It was sky blue. Underneath they found another one. It was sunny yellow!

Lake picked up that one and another one was underneath! He picked one after another until there was none left.

The others were ocean aqua, fire red, grassy green and earthy orange.

'They're the diamonds of nature,' said Journey, really excited.

When they got back to their boat, they told their parents everything. It really was a wonderful island.

Photo Competition

By Eva S.

The feeling of the salty breeze warmed Jessica's skin as she captured photos on the giant cruise boat. She had to win the prize. She was determined to win. Photography was her passion. Jessica didn't have many friends, the only comfort she found was in her photos. She wanted to show her parents she was good at photography and shouldn't go to medical school.

Bang! The cruise ship hit the island. An announcement shortly followed over the loudspeaker, 'We need to make some repairs to the boat. Natasha will take you on a tour.'

As Jessica leapt onto the sand, she glanced around the desolate island and excitedly thought, *these will be the most unique, prize-winning photos.*

Click, click, click, Jessica was euphoric. Capturing the mysterious island she was in her happy place. While she was busy taking photos, she didn't realise the tour group was still walking until it was too late. No matter how fast she ran, she couldn't catch up. In the distance, she suddenly heard the boat engine grow loud and realised they were leaving! Jessica chased after them in vain. She hoped they would come back but they didn't. To make things worse she had no internet and her phone was flat. She tried yelling but the boat was too far away. Having a quiet voice didn't help either. She wondered how she would ever get home or survive on the island. She had to find some shelter for the night. It was getting dark. If only she wasn't so distracted with the photos she was taking. She thought, *what if I never find a way home?* She began to lose hope as she fell asleep on the hard rocky ground.

The next morning she woke to the feeling of water splashing on her. Someone had come. She was so relieved. She started screaming, 'Over here!'

A man came up to her.

'Who are you?' asked Jessica with confusion. He didn't answer. Her mind was swirling with questions.

A few minutes later she was on the back of his jet ski. She was asking him questions about how he found her.

He explained that he found her photos on the boat and knew which tour boat she would have been on.

Later that week, when she was safely home, Jessica received an email saying that she had won a trip to a mysterious island as a photography prize.

The Treasure of the Gods

By Federico M.

Legend tells of the mighty Captain Crow and his search for the Treasure of the Gods. A treasure so large, they say, that it was beyond a man's wildest dreams. All Crow and his men had to do was make it past the dark seas and they would find themselves in Paradise. They were never seen again.

Walking on the beach, Ethan tried to forget the day he had experienced at school. Kicking the sand, something flashed in Ethan's eye. It was a bottle with a piece of paper rolled up inside. It was a map—a treasure map to the Treasure of the Gods.

Ethan ran to his best friend's house to tell Max about the map, but Max didn't believe it was real. So, Ethan told Max about Captain Crow's final voyage, convincing his friend the map and the treasure were real.

Secretly borrowing Max's dad's boat, the two friends set sail for the dark seas.

'Hey, Max, do you think we will make it?' asked Ethan.

'Of course!' said Max, pointing to the horizon, 'look! What's that over there?'

'We've made it to the dark seas!' Ethan yelled.

Whoosh! Whoosh! Gigantic waves smashed against the boat. Clouds appeared out of nowhere, surrounding the two friends. Boom! Alone in the middle of nowhere, Ethan and

Max were hit by a massive wave.

Washed up on the shore, Ethan woke with his face in the sand, 'What, where are we?' Ethan looked at his surroundings. 'Max, Max! Wake up! I think we've arrived!'

Following the map, the two friends headed into the jungle. They searched everywhere. Every tree, every hole, every coconut, but they couldn't find any treasure.

Unable to find the treasure and realising their boat had been destroyed in the storm, Max stomped angrily on the sand. A hollow sound echoed his stomp. Thump! Thump! Thump!

They dug as fast as they could until, suddenly, the sand gave way and the two friends found themselves falling. Splash! They fell into the water.

Gasping for air, they realised they were in a large cave. Their jaws dropped as they stared at Captain Crow's lost ship.

Climbing aboard, they searched the old boat. Hidden below deck was the fabled Treasure of the Gods. Laughing hysterically, the two friends hugged each other with joy. They had their treasure, a ship to sail home, and they'd had the adventure of a lifetime!

Refuge

By Thys vR

Her flaxen hair whipped in the wind and the rain lashed her eyes as a string of foul profanities erupted from her lips when she felt the throttle jam. Crunch. The boat bucked and lurched beneath her as a jagged rock pierced its hull. Unable to keep her feet any longer, she lost her hold on the wheel and tumbled over board, shrieking curses all the while. The water dragged her beneath the surface and filled her nose and mouth as the current pulled her onwards. Her breath exploded out of her as she hit a rock concealed by the gloom. Desperate now, she flailed blindly, scrabbling for any purchase she could get. Out of air, her eyes began to flutter and the current pulled her onward.

Spitting out a mouthful of sand, she took stock of her surroundings, turning her back to the gentle lapping of the waves and gazing at the vast expanse of green before her. Birds twittered and monkeys howled before they were silenced by a thunderous roar. With a dazed shrug she looked down at the tattered attire she was wearing, noting a battered band of silver clinging to her finger in the shape of an eagle taking flight. 'Artemis,' she whispered bemusedly, reading the tag stuck to her chest, 'must be my name.'

Artemis groaned as the shadows lengthened. She gazed

at her day's work, a raft lashed together with the thickest vines she could find. It wasn't much but it would have to do.

As she progressed further into the ocean a storm abruptly exploded. Waves climbed high and crashed onto her raft that creaked as the vines strained to keep the scavenged driftwood logs together. Artemis swallowed her terror as a sudden shadow burst from the depths. As it flailed on the raft, its beady eyes of onyx focused on her. A pained screech burst from her as the thing's jaws latched onto her leg. Crunch! Artemis screamed again when the beast's maw snapped her leg. Blind with tears of pain and fear she clutched the rudder as the beast tried to drag her below the surface. Desperately, her other leg kicked out, slamming into the creature's nose. It released the leg with a pained bellow, slipping back into the depths. She sobbed and panted as the raft burst free of the storm.

Secondary (Years 7-10) Category

Sandy's Beach

By Maddie Lyn

Stars of sunlight bounce and glitter off the ocean, winking at me, daring me to enter. I can smell the salt on the breeze, feel the sand on my toes, and see and hear the ocean, the huge beautiful dangerous ocean. I finally feel at peace, a deep sense of contentment seeping into my bones. All of my problems ooze into the sand, waiting patiently for me to regain them when I leave the island.

'Leigh, are you going to help me unpack?' Sandy calls from the small buggy that drove us to the resort.

I shake off my daydreaming as I walk over to her, my university roommate.

Sandy looks as if she was made for this beach, with her shining golden hair, her flawless golden skin, and eyes as green as beer bottle shards that wash up on the beach. Maybe that's why I like her so much. She reminds me of the beach.

I'm different. I look like I was made of night, with my inky black hair and my grey eyes, so out of place with the shining beach, but I feel at home all the same.

After we had unpacked, Sandy and I chucked on our togs and

went to the beach for a quick swim before dinner. There were some people down on the beach, but not many. I had heard the manager of the resort tell us to stay by the pool, but Sandy and I weren't good at following the rules. As we were leaving the beach, I swear the sand in my shoes felt heavy, weighing me down, wanting me to stay. Sandy trailed behind me, winging about how heavy the sand in her shoes felt too.

The crashing waves soon lulled me to sleep. The next morning, Sandy and I got up for breakfast. Lots of people must have left as the few that had been around here seemed to have disappeared. How strange, I thought, but at least we had this whole place to ourselves.

When we finally got down to the beach, we lathered on sunscreen. Sandy flicked water on my back causing ripples of goose bumps on my skin. Together we played some beach cricket with the bats and balls we had found abandoned on the way down here.

After resting and sunbaking for a while, I dug my fingers into the sand. I nearly jumped out of my skin. I stood upright, shock and confusion twisting in my mind. The sand was vibrating.

'Are you okay? What happened? Did something bite you?' Sandy sprayed me with questions.

Unable to focus on her, I sat back down digging my hands back into the sand, trying not to squeal when yet again I felt the vibration. But this time it felt like words. I stayed seated and tried to focus on them. They sounded like static.

'Don't leave ... stay ... no one ... comes ... here ... anymore ...'

I pulled my hands out of the sand and the sounds stopped. Was the island speaking to me? Sandy was still watching me with concern in her eyes. 'Sandy, this sounds crazy, but I think the island is speaking to me.'

She just looked at me, then burst out laughing. 'That's funny stuff, Leigh. You should ...' but she was cut off when she began to seep into the sand, her feet disappeared, then her ankles and shins.

Then I started to sink too. The sand was swallowing us up.

'Forever ... Sandy ... must ... stay.'

'This isn't fun. We will die and then no one will visit you!' I yelled to the sand, praying that it would let us go.

The sand began to ease us both back to the surface. I kept eye contact with Sandy as we rose. The moment we were finally released, I glanced at the resort and mouthed, NOW. We both bolted off the beach, leaving all our belongings behind.

The water followed us up the beach, the high tide coming in much faster than it should have. The waves were trying to catch us.

'What did the sand say to you, Leigh? What did you hear?' Sandy whispered.

'The beach is lonely. It wants you to stay,' I whispered back. Then it dawned on me. 'You don't think that's where all the other people went?' I questioned Sandy, hoping she could tell me that I was just being silly.

Grief swallowed the beauty of her green eyes. 'How are we going to get off?' she asked.

I started pacing, thinking deeply. I think a storm may be brewing. 'Come!' I shouted. 'Out to the docks! I will bribe them to take us before the storm hits.'

We ran towards the docks. When we arrived, we found that the docks were gone, swallowed by the rising tide.

Grief and understanding suffocated my heart. 'There's no way off, Sandy,' I said and she wrapped her arms around me as the island swallowed us whole.

Their Foreign Island

By Neve G.

When I die, will my body be buried or will it be left to decay wherever I fall? Will my soul drift back to where my ancestors are laid? Or will I forever be bound to this foreign land?

I don't understand their language. My tongue doesn't wrap around words as theirs do. But I don't need to understand what they're saying. They think we are stupid because we do not live like they do; talk like they do; look like they do.

I've grown used to the hollow feeling of hunger. Boiled potatoes and salted beef are as foreign to me as their language. My island dreaming fills the ache in my stomach and soothes my tortured soul. But those moments are fleeting, and the void is constant.

Sometimes I'll capture my reflection in the small pools left behind by the rarity of rain. I don't recognise the girl who looks back up at me. Her hair is coarse and falling out in places. Her cheeks are gaunt and eyes hollow. Her dark collar bones stick out from under her torn shirt and a pallor assaults her sable skin. It's poetic how I reflect this land, these people.

Without giving me a moment to shed the sleep from my brain, to allow me to live in the bliss of being half awake and forgetful, I was shaken awake by a familiar face. *Charlie*. At the sight of him a smile began to tug on my lips but quickly loosened when I noticed his narrowed brows and clenched jaw. His usually affectionate eyes glistened with tears, and he drew his lower lip between his teeth as he crouched down beside me.

Panic clawed at my stomach causing me to sit up and face him. *Not again.* The air here was thick and heavy, every intake of breath like a hand reaching down your throat and strangling your lungs. He didn't have to say a word for me to know why he had woken me up before call. I saw it in his eyes, I heard it in his breath. Moonlight streamed through a lonely window, its light exposing the damp earthen floors, casting shadows on his tortured features.

'Show me,' I whispered.

He seemed to argue with this idea in his head before giving me a rigid nod.

I followed him as he stood and crept outside, then vanished into the darkness.

Charlie was not his true name. It was the label the recruiters gave him. I'd asked his name once and he had only shrugged. He told me it didn't matter anymore; his name was Charlie now and that was that.

Outside the air was swollen with the smell of smouldering fires. The grass on my soles was prickly and coarse, a gentle tickle as I followed Charlie deeper into the grassland. Occasional trees, twisted and gnarled, dotted the landscape. It was as though they too wanted to uproot themselves and run away from this land. The new moon cast its guiding light, revealing the sugarcane that covered almost every inch of the land as far as the eye could see, waiting to be hacked at sunrise and shipped off to places overseas.

I didn't notice Charlie had stopped until I nearly ran into his back. He stood as unmoving as a rock. His eyes pinned on something in front of him I could not see. I found his hand in the darkness and gripped it tightly as I moved past him. My heart sank. I have learned to show no response to pain, physical or emotional. But it never gets easier. I can never stop the throbbing agony of my heart, each ache a whisper into my ear. *You failed.*

The man on the grass didn't look dead. If it weren't for his stilled chest, I would have thought he was merely resting. His eyes were closed, his hands rested gently on the grass. Beside him lay his over-worked sickle and bundles of sugar cane, evidence of his toil since dawn. His features had softened, uncharacteristically so, normally tortured in this Island prison, but so different in death, peaceful even. A small smile played on his thin dead lips, and I realised my growing envy. His soul had drifted back to where our ancestors lay, his body forever bound to this foreign land. He had returned home the only way he could have, the only way they'd let us.

The Social Islands

By V. Rook

Definition of island: (2.) a thing regarded as resembling an island, especially in being isolated, detached, or surrounded in some way.

Aaron has ataxic cerebral palsy. His home is defined by his wheelchair, and his family are like his nurses. Aaron is non-verbal and will never be able to experience the joys and wonders of life like most kids; however, he is considered one of the lucky ones. As the doctors greyly put it, 'His intellectual ability is unblemished.'

Aaron knew that this was meant to be a positive sign, but all he could feel was numbness and emptiness inside. *'It doesn't make a difference at all's all,'* he thought. *'I still won't be able to speak or move. After all, what is the point of thoughts and opinions if not to share.'* Aaron was transferred from his wheelchair to his bed, where he was laid back. That night he closed his eyes, and entered the land of his unconsciousness-his dreams.

Aaron dreamt of the pristine sand that waited for him on the island. His island was substantial, undivided and all his. He didn't have to share his joy, he could run and swim and walk as he soaked up the sun. In his island he could speak and talk to the trees. But what he loved most was the anarchic, unruly waves of the beach.

Aaron was awoken by his parents. They both sat on his bed and talked to him, despite the fact that Aaron couldn't respond. For this, he was grateful. It made him feel somewhat included.

'Aaron, we haven't taken you outside for a while,' His mother recalled.' And Aunt May is having a family reunion. I think that this will be a perfect opportunity to reconnect with family.' This caught Aaron by surprise, as he couldn't even remember the last time he had seen his family.

Aaron dozed off to his island once again … quite ironic in truth, Aaron feels like an island: so inaccessible, remote and isolated. He never feels understood, like he is just defined by his wheelchair and cerebral palsy, which isn't exactly incorrect.

In his island as he is soaking up the sun, and bobbing in the waves, Aaron discerns an inky body of land beyond the reef, illuminated by sparkles of light. Although his island is beautiful and alluring, Aaron longs to be connected with the main land. Soon all he can conceptualise is life connected with people that understand him.

All morning he wondered what it would be like to finally see his family. Aaron thought about what it would be like to make friends and experience normalcy like every other kid. For hours he thought about this and with every passing thought, his hopes rose.

Later that day, he was wheeled out to the car and awkwardly strapped into his seat. He thought about his island dreams. *'Maybe today is the day I can sail to the mainland. The day I can finally connect with people.'* If only he knew how wrong he'd be.

His Father came to the car door, lifted him out of the

sturdy seat, and secured him into his wheelchair. He grasped the handlebars and pushed Aaron out with heavy steps. Aaron sensed that his father was nervous.

They went inside the house, his wheels squeaking every few steps. As they headed towards the light inside, Aaron related this experience to sailing across the dividing ocean, becoming adjacent to the mainland. But oh how he was misled. Turns out that this experience is more adjoining his small sailing boat sinking. As he entered the room, he was met with gasps and stares from children and adults.

Aaron didn't mind though. Instead he observed the room and surveyed the people in there. Children selfishly entitling themselves to food despite the fact that there were others that needed to be fed. Mothers handing their children technology to shut them up. Children taking their lives and privileges for granted. All of the little things that people underestimate. As he observed the room, he could tell that people pitied him. After an hour of this event, they went home in silence.

Later that night, as Aaron sat on his island, it was illuminated to him how lucky he was to be protected from all the filth and sickness in the world. His disability has separated him from the rest. Although it appears that he is the one with sickness, it is others that have the sickened mind, drowning in their own entitlement.

How fortunate he was to have the vast ocean that, in a way, opened up another perception and aspect of gratitude in him. And although Aaron will never have what is considered a 'normal' life, he will always have his island dreams.

Stranded

By Kayla A.

The warm ocean air ruffled the waves and blew his hair across his face. Bright sunlight glittered over the water. The hazy silhouette of a lush island flickered on the horizon. That was where he was headed. This island had the best fishing grounds in all the reef. He came here every year. But this year it was different.

The skies darkened. Dark storm clouds raced at his back, and with them came icy winds and wild seas. He pushed the throttle and the boat surged forwards. He wasn't going to make it to the island in time. At that moment, the storm overtook him.

The waves rose around him, bigger than sand dunes in the driest desert. The nose of the boat reared as it climbed a wave. He braced himself against the dash as the boat crested the wave and plunged downwards, picking up speed.

The island was closer now, only a few kilometers away. He was almost there. He glanced up to check the sun, but it was nowhere to be seen. Blue sky flickered in and out of sight from under the fast-moving cloud cover.

He cried out as the boat suddenly stopped. His forehead slammed into the windscreen and his vision blurred. Through his distorted vision he could make out what the throw of water had exposed. A deadly mountain of jagged rock lay in front of him. It was covered in algae that glistened in the dappled sunshine like the light from a thousand stars. The boat shuddered. He fell to the floor and the darkness became absolute.

When he came to it was still daylight. The sunlight felt like an iron spike being thrust between his eyes. He got up with a groan as a wave slammed into the side of the boat. A grinding sound made him jump. The boat was still on the rocks. Realization hit him like a shockwave. The boat had hit the rocks and it was now shipwrecked.

The tide was rising, and he needed to float the boat, or it would be completely submerged. He threw the heavier items out of the boat. The boat became lighter, and it shifted on the rocks. He pushed the rock with the spare oar and the boat floated free.

He dragged a canvas sheet across the bottom of the boat to try to stop the seawater from flooding the hull. The engine roared and the boat shot forward. He turned it sharply towards the island. He could already feel the boat slowing down as seawater seeped through the canvas. He hoped it would last until he reached the island.

A rumbling noise made him turn. Another boat was coming towards him at full speed. He hastily clambered onto the roof and stood, waving his arms. 'Help,' he cried. 'Help, I'm sinking!' He waved and jumped and screamed, but the boat continued past. He slumped in despair. His boat had taken in so much water it was beginning to sink. There was no way it was going to make it to the island.

The boat rocked violently in the waves. He stumbled. The currents had brought the sinking boat even closer to the island. But it was not close enough. He was still over a kilometre away and he couldn't swim. He scrabbled for a flare and and shot it just as the floor lurched from under him.

His life jacket snagged on the handrail and was ripped off. He fell and splashed into the ocean. He grasped fruitlessly at the slick hull and felt himself sinking. He tried to tread water. The boat was almost swamped by a wave and lurched towards him. He pushed himself away, choking on salt water. Salt burned his throat as he sank below the churning waves. He could just make out schools of iridescent fish dancing around the coral far below. Anemone swayed in the gentle currents.

He didn't know how long he stared at the sea life, mesmerised by their beauty. He only knew that they were gone now, and the reef was deserted. The blue sky winked at him through the dappled waves. A seagull lifted and flew away. He was alone now.

His lungs ached for air as he struggled towards the surface. A stuttering roar reached his ears. Above the surface a great dark shadow took form. It was long and wide and roared. As it neared him, a rope splashed beside him. His thrashing arms grasped the lifeline and he hauled himself to the surface. His breath rattled in his lungs and his racing heart slowed. Unknown hands grabbed his and pulled him onto the boat. He flopped on the deck curling in on himself, coughing until his throat was raw. A blanket was thrown over him as the boat gunned it towards the island.

They passed shoals, reefs, and schools of fish. The water brightened from deep blue to turquoise as the soft sand shifted in the waves. The boat surfed onto the shore.

He stumbled over the side of the boat and collapsed on the sand, overcome by fatigue. His arms shook as he dragged himself over the hot shifting sand. He could hear people yelling in the distance. Their cries assaulted his ears as they drew nearer. But it was all right. He would be safe now.

Chronicles of an Island

By Georgie Z.

Cerulean waves crashed onto my sandy beaches. Shells and rocks were being drawn in and out. Palm trees were littered across my back. Butterflies flittered around every nook and cranny. But one thing was missing … Humans.

Eventually, they did find me. I was shocked that they had never come across me before. Humans had always been too arrogant and overconfident to care about little bits of land like me. I was not a part of a country yet. Anyone could try and take me as theirs.

First, a large country that I cannot remember the name of, claimed me. I remember them flocking to me, women in bikinis sunbathing on towels and men swimming in the ocean. Then one day, they stopped coming. Rumour has it that the country had been wiped out by other humans who were jealous of them. I found it very strange. I would never try to destroy an island just because I was envious of them.

The next humans who came were quite different. Instead of swimwear, these people wore apparel worthy of the explorers I hear other islands whisper about. They would take a shell here, capture a bug there, and everything in between.

I did not like them. They took too much.

One day, while the humans were collecting things, a boat

appeared near my shore. The men on board were holding weapons, dressed head to toe in tactical gear. They came and they did terrible things to the other humans. I heard one of the awful men say to another, 'Those scientists won't have a home if they go back anyway. Boss said their home has been blown up.'

For the next few years, I'm not quite sure how long exactly, the humans continued like this. People would try to make me a part of their country, then a jealous one would come and blow them up. It started a war among those countries that were left.

The other islands whispered things to me, saying they knew humans would start something called 'WW3.' Soon, it wasn't just me that was a fuel for their chaos. They wanted to take each other over. It was a competition to see who could get the most land, the most power.

Bombs continued to fly over my head and, often, humans would flock to me and hide amongst the palm trees. Eventually, another group of humans would find them, and they would battle. Slowly, the sky turned from a soft baby blue to a smoky haze that masked the colour of fire that flamed across the sky. The countries that surrounded me were slowly burning, smog rising above these blackened countries. Of course, people would sometimes come to me and try to claim me as their own, but they continued to fight because of jealousy and greed.

One day, a silence fell over the land. Complete silence. The palm trees that were scattered ever so generously throughout my land were pushed out of their sockets. Butterflies and ladybugs fell gracefully into the grass. The quiet screams of other islands rang out around me. It all happened quickly, softly, sadly. Silently.

Everything was gone. The loud noise that was made by humans had vanished and every living creature on Earth was gone.

The world continued to burn around me, black smoke drifting its way into the atmosphere. The burning colour of the world made it impossible to tell where the land ended, and the sky began. The grass that covered most of me began to burn until not even it was left. And the saddest thing of all, my once beautiful, blue water was full of ash and debris, turning it black, a colour that reflected all the islands' mood. Everything was gone. Everything had been taken from us. The paradise had now been stripped of everything because of selfishness and greed.

I looked at the dying world before I closed my eyes. There was no longer a need for me to exist. I was no longer an asset to Earth. I was supposed to be a gift to them. Instead, they took too much. They knew it would end like this. Some were less selfish than others, but really, every human was responsible in their own way. Now, they will pay. So will I. The other islands, animals, plants, and the sea, they all feel the pain.

The humans were gone in a second, but we will die a sad, slow death, disintegrating into the core of the Earth, the sky ringing out with our never-ending screams. We suffer. We knew we would have to suffer the most in the end.

The Tale of the Brave Little Island

Micaela T.

It was the worst storm that Little Island had ever seen. CRASH! White-hot lightning struck overhead. BOOM! The thunder replied, splitting the sky in two with an unearthly crashing of symbols. An endless torrent of rain bucketed down on Little Island's back. The seas roared all around her, drowning her in staggeringly tall waves, roughly pushing her and kicking her.

She felt her already feeble grip on the muddy seafloor loosen. She tried to shout for help, but she was dragged underwater by a strong rip which swept her into deep waters. Little Island had never felt more frightened in all her five years of life. She fought desperately, but to no avail. Her head knocked on a rock and she lost consciousness, letting the ocean sweep her away ...

Hot sunlight blared overhead, but the water where Little Island bobbed around was chilly and cold. She shivered. Where was she? Little Island felt like crying. She didn't know where she was, or how she was going to get back to her family.

'Ahoy there!' Little Island heard someone shout.

She spun around, searching for the owner of the voice. In

the distance, she saw a tiny boat approaching her.

'Ahoy there!' it shouted again.

'Hello!' Little Island replied.

As the boat got closer, she could see that it was a small fishing boat. It was a bit worse for wear, with fading green paint and a sputtering motor, but it was still cheerfully puffing out smoke from one of its funnels.

'Lost at sea, are you?' the boat asked politely.

'Yes,' she whispered, a lump stuck in her throat. 'Do you know where I am?' she inquired.

The boat stopped near one of the small reefs that surrounded her. 'Yah, you're in the Tasman Sea, a bit of a way off the coast of Auckland,' the boat nodded solemnly.

When she heard this, Little Island felt her heart drop into her stomach. She knew in that instant that she was further away from home than she'd ever been before.

'New Zealand?' she squeaked.

The boat nodded again, 'Yup. Where do you hail from anyways?'

'Livingstone Shire, in Australia,' Little Island replied faintly.

The fishing boat whistled, long and low. 'Gee, you're a bit of a way from home,' it commented.

Little Island gulped. 'I know. A storm blew me away, and I need to get back. Do you know the way?' she asked nervously.

The small fishing boat puffed out smoke rings as it thought. 'Well,' it said after a while, 'I'm an old boat and my memory ain't so good these days, but I remember that if you go in a north-westerly line from here, you'll end up at Livingstone Shire.' The old boat wheezed and coughed. 'I gotta get going now. Afternoon, Miss.' It nodded to Little Island and puttered away.

Little Island stared after it for a while, then suddenly started scrambling after the boat as if snapping out of a trance. 'Wait!' she panicked, trying to catch up to it, but the boat was too fast, and she was too slow. The fishing boat was already a speck in the distance. With one final wheeze it disappeared altogether, leaving Little Island alone again.

'Please wait,' Little Island mumbled, sadly looking in the direction that it had gone, 'I still need you.'

* * *

'North-ways and west-ways,' Little Island chanted, using the magnetic pull of the north and south poles as a makeshift compass to guide her. She had been travelling for a few days now, and slowly the water was getting *slightly* warmer. She was still too short to reach the bottom of the sea, so she'd been swimming instead, and she was getting rather tired. After a long time, Little Island reached a point where she could stand on the seafloor. After that the journey was much quicker and happier.

'Do you know how far away Australia is?' Little Island often inquired of the sea life that she passed.

'Soon, soon!' they replied, cheering her on.

* * *

One warm sunny day, Little Island was slowly dragging her feet forwards and was feeling very sorry for herself, when she saw a familiar looking coastline in front of her, stretching for as far as she could see. Little Island's heart pounded and immediately she knew who it was. 'Mama!' she cried, sprinting towards Australia as fast as she could.

Australia turned and they embraced tightly. 'You must have had a big adventure!' Australia grinned.

You have no idea, Little Island thought as she looked up at her mother.

Australia took her daughter's hand. 'Let's get you safely back with your siblings,' she said.

Little Island smiled up at her. 'I'm so grateful to be home again,' she sighed softly.

Secondary (Years 11-12) Category

Stories by the Sea

By Sharona U.

Many moons ago, in the middle of the ocean, I was the most beautiful island to rise from the sea floor. An environmental masterpiece they'd call me, with my beautiful beaches and soft sand. The way the breeze made my palm leaves shiver was always so graceful. I was breathtaking. I was the home for lovely native plants, happy animals and important resources. Nothing could ever change the cycle of my life.

Many years later, things began to evolve. My children began to get bigger and grow. They were wearing strange pieces of material around their bodies now and communicating in an unfamiliar way. They were killing off my animals and consuming them, and cutting all the trees down to make shelter for themselves. I don't understand why they would do that. I thought my jungle was protection enough.

I must punish them somehow, I thought. *I can't just let them do this to me and everything I've worked so hard for.*

So, I thought I should come up with some kind of disaster, a flood maybe. I hoped this would teach them a lesson.

But what's this? I saw odd looking trees floating on the water. They looked as if they had white apes aboard. *That's so strange,* I thought. *Where did they come from?*

They floated towards me, and I could see my people running and scattering into the bushes, they were just as afraid as I was.

As time went on, more and more white apes came to my shores, stealing my people and my animals, cutting my trees and plants down, and constructing such weird monuments. They built reinforced walls along my beachside to prevent my water from rising too high.

Every night after these strange people came, I could hear my children crying, screaming. It broke my heart. These strangers had no care for me or my creations.

Years have gone by. I don't see many of my children anymore. Most of them have been taken over the sea on logs with cloth like material above. If I'm lucky, I'll see some of their faces, so happy to escape before being captured again. I don't know what these people want from me, or them. They're kids. They don't know any better than to run when they're scared or fight back when they're feeling brave. Why are they being punished?

More time has gone by and now I see one of my children grown up. She speaks to her people. It looks as if she's trying to convince them to do something crazy. I hope she doesn't hurt herself, or any of my other children. She's always had so much resilience, that girl. She was only ten when the white apes came. She led all the children into a cave when they arrived and, ever since, she has been planning her attack. What a brave young lady. Always thinking about others.

Night fell. I was awakened by the screams of not my children but the white apes! My little girl has begun to fight back. She's burned their monuments to the ground and chased the apes away. My children are safe now. But I'm damaged. I have no jungle anymore; I have man-made debris all over me. Some of this debris is killing off my friends that swim around me and it's not just hurting me but my family and friends. Again, nothing can be done. But I have my children and now they're safe once again.

What's this? Why are my children acting this way. What have they brought here? Why is there so much plastic? Have my children adapted these habits from those horrid white monsters? I guess so. How could they do this to me? After everything I have done for them. I gave them life; I have provided for them since the beginning of my time, and this is how they repay me? Why is there so much smog choking my lungs. Plastic is filling my best friend, the sea, killing all her children.

This horrific turn of events is sickening. One minute it's hot, the next is cold, the world around me is polluted. My friends and family are dying slowly. People are coming and going as they please. It's not fair. How did this come to be? I can't live on like this. What my children are doing is killing me. My beautiful beaches are now tarred roads. My graceful palm trees are no longer there. It's not fair.

I now know what I must do. And though my children may not approve, it must be done. I will go back down to my old home, back into the sea, where I'll be safe. Goodbye my children. I know that you can become better than you are now. Stay safe. I love you.

The Islands of Giants

By Elijah A.

My arms were weary. I sat on a small outcrop overlooking the Islands of the Giants. I had found myself transported to this realm during a battle with an old nemesis, Ulf. He caused me to stumble on a teleportation rune that propelled me through the Bifrost and onto the islands. I was, of course, enraged by my humiliating defeat. I knew that I would get my revenge in due time.

The second I landed, I was confronted by the island's natives. They were unhappy with my sudden presence in their sacred land and attempted to kill me. So I disposed of them. I located a temple that could teleport me back to where I was originally but it was, unfortunately, situated on top of the mountain I was climbing. With an exhausted sigh I tightened my blade to my side and began to climb once more.

My name is Gorm. I was on a journey to a dwarven mine, with the aim of strengthening my blade with their enchantments and steel. In Midgard I was ambushed by my nemesis Ulf, who is much weaker than me, but more cunning and deceptive. He had been my nemesis since I shattered his strength rune. He had planned to use this on himself to invade his brother's kingdom and usurp the throne. I had been hired by his brother, the king, to stop Ulf's invasion and, of course, I was victorious. But now I continue to climb, the rage of my recent defeat still burning fresh in my mind.

I had reached a problem in my ascent. Above me was a horizontal overhang that extended three meters and surrounded the mountain like a ring on a finger. There was no way to climb around it, or over it due to its unnaturally smooth surface. Even with my brute strength, my arms were beginning to tire and I could feel them slip from my hold on the mountain. I steadied my left arm and lowered my right arm slowly to my belt, where I drew my blade. It was about seventy centimetres long, comprised of dwarven steel and elven silver with drops of sap from the World Tree.

I had acquired my blade in a journey through Midgard where I had come upon it stuck inside a boulder covered with vines and moss. The second I touched it, it sprung from the stone into my hand, forever binding itself to me. From then on, I used it to help me battle many enemies and always victorious. The dwarven blacksmiths who crafted the blade, told me of its materials and other-worldly powers. They alone were the ones who could alter the blade. These were the dwarves I was journeying to see when I was interrupted by Ulf.

A sudden gust of ocean wind interrupted my daydreaming and I refocused, remembering the powers of the blade. I brought the blade up and cut along the smooth surface of the ledge above. The blade cut through effortlessly. I sheathed my sword and dug my fingers into the gouge I had created on the ledge. I was able to get enough purchase to raise my left arm into another hold. I repeated this tactic until I was at the very end of the ledge.

I looked down and saw the bodies of the island natives that I had disposed of earlier. They were now specs on the sandy beach. I steeled myself and grabbed around the smooth side of the ledge, vainly attempting to continue my ascent. Suddenly, I felt a strange, furry hand grabbing tightly around my forearm and within seconds I was effortlessly lifted. I flew and smashed onto the rocky surface of the ledge.

Dazed, I wearily got up and looked over to the masculine, hairy figure before me. Eight-feet tall, with the torso of a wolf, he stood on two legs with sculpted human features and an oily, midnight black coat which appeared to provide him with protection against projectiles. His fiery red eyes burned a hole through me. I realised his intent was malevolent rather than saving me from the ledge.

I drew my blade and it hummed in my hand. A silver mist exited the runes on the sword's blade surrounding it in a silver storm. The creature saw this and charged, its muscles propelling him forwards at an alarming rate. I placed my left hand on the hilt and swung the sword to the left, slicing across his face.

His momentum knocked my sword out of my hand and pinned me to the ground.

I felt the creature's massive hand enclose my waist as it raised me above his head. I grabbed its fingers, and the creature loosened its grip. I took this brief fortuitous moment to release myself from its grip and army rolled, coming to a stop right next to my sword. I heard the wolf get off the ground and I grabbed my sword and charged. I plunged my blade into the dazed creature's chest. I then grabbed the hilt and tore the sword to the side. As my blade exited its body, the creature fell to its knees and dropped heavily to the ground. I brushed the dust off my shoulder as I sheathed my sword.

I surveyed my surroundings. The temple was covered with vines and the entrance was overgrown. I stepped over the body of the wolf and scanned the ground as I approached the steps, looking for runic traps.

I ascended the steps that led to the entrance and went

through. I was greeted by the sight of a large antechamber, and in the middle lay an old stone archway. It was covered with different runes and other magical symbols. I found a stone pedestal that had a singular rune engraved in the top. I wiped away some vines and moss and put my hand on the rune. I closed my eyes and called out, 'I ask for the power of the Bifrost oh Heimdall, and that you lend a mere mortal like me a fraction of your vast power to return me back to my realm so that I may continue my journey'.

As if on cue, a rainbow beam came through the top of the temple and fell upon the archway. I always loved pretending to praise the Gods. A waterfall of blue energy ignited in the archway and fell into a swirling whirlpool that grew until it encompassed the archway.

I smiled at the thought of my sweet revenge as I stepped into the archway. I felt a feeling of weightlessness as I was traveling through the Yggdrasil. Finally, back to my realm. The weightlessness subsided as my feet felt solid ground and my blade began to hum.

The Heart of Tafari

By Jasmine F.

For hundreds of years, the island has been inhabited by people showing off her beautiful scenery when the sun rose and fell. She provided resources for us in her clear waters that were swimming with life, and in the dewy forests that burst with the sound of drums beating and families singing. The beating of the drums was an imitation of the island's mighty heartbeat.

There was always peace among those who lived here. Everyone knew each other and everyone was family. During the day, the children helped the villagers building huts and learned how to hunt for food in the water and the forests. During the night, the elders of the village would gather all the children around the fire and tell them stories of their ancestors.

On this particular night, the village elder told the children one of the island's oldest fable, the Tale of the Heart of Tafari.

'Many years ago, our ancestors found a large cave under the island while hunting in the water. They believed that cave held the heart of the island. There was a myth that anyone who held the heart of the island in their hand could have the power to manipulate the sea.'

The children surrounding were awed, imagining what the heart of the island looked like. The tale telling drew in a crowd of nearby villagers.

'The chief of the village had gathered everyone around and announced that a small group of villagers, including himself, were going to find the heart and use its power. The chief would keep his people happy and provide everything they needed to survive, although he didn't do it in the right way.

Our chief had become a foe of the neighbouring island. The feud between them had been going on for almost a year by then. The leader of the neighbouring island had always done everything he could to antagonise our own, whether it was hunting the fish in our side of the bay, cutting the netting of our fish nets or stealing our crab pots and taking whatever was inside. Our chief had had enough of their antics. He wanted to use the heart to summon a tsunami so large; it would wipe out his foe. The other villagers were shocked that he wanted to do something so despicable. They started asking questions ... What about the innocent villagers over there? Women and children ... What will happen after they are wiped out? Can't we make some sort of peace; this is far too—

The chief had silenced them with a booming roar ... "ENOUGH! ALL OF YOU! I am doing this for our families! Our children! OUR ISLAND! They are stealing our food, destroying our pots and netting! I will not stand for this; I am your chieftain! It is my duty to keep you all alive and if they keep taking food from us then the island alone may not be able to provide for us. Her forests may be able to yield berries and fruits for us now, but it won't last. We will run out."

The villagers had submitted to their chief. He had manipulated them into thinking that he was doing this for the good of their own survival. He knew that they'd agree with him that way.

A few days later, the chief gathered a group of three

other men and set off towards the underside of the island. After hours of climbing mountains, walking non-stop and sliding down hillsides, they came to a cliffside leading down to the beach on the north-eastern side of the island. The chief turned to the men, "The caves entrance is down there to the left," he said. "We haven't been inside this cave before, so we need to be on guard for any danger, understood?"

A series of nods from the men followed the chief's words. They set off towards the caves entrance.

The chief was smirking. He'd finally be able to win this feud. He could draft a tsunami and destroy their island. The chief began to think of all the things he could do and he hadn't even found the heart of Tafari yet.

After another hour of wandering, one of the men stopped, holding up the others.

"What is it?" The chief asked.

The man pointed further ahead and that's when the chief saw it. A pulsating glow coming from a further pathway. "The heart is in there!"

The chief bolted down that path, only halting when he saw the very heart of his island. Jogging to the wall the jewel was imbedded in, he wrapped his hand around it and pulled with all his might. The jewel budged and abandoned its confines in the stone wall. "The power of the sea is at my mercy!" The chief raised his arms high victoriously.

With the heart and his men with him, the chief walked back to the village. Once they reached the village, the chief held up the heart and those who agreed with him, cheered and roared.

The next day, the chief and his men stood on the edge of the beach, facing the enemy island. With the heart in his hand, the chief summoned a tsunami wave that towered over the island and crashed into it. The wave rushed through their forest and their village, leaving nothing but wreckage that couldn't be fixed. The chief was so fixated on revenge that he had no mercy for those who inhabited the island. All he wanted was to wipe out those against him.

The chief was satisfied. He was happy that his men were bringing in more food and there were no more damaged nets or pots. But after a week, terrible cyclones brought terror to the island, drowning all crops with rain, scaring away the fish and washing aside their pots. The storms lasted for days.

There were rumours spreading around the village that the balance of nature was unsettled, and that the chief had cursed the island. When the chief heard of the rumours, he started to worry. Everything the villagers were saying seemed true and he couldn't let his people suffer. He had sworn to protect them, so at nightfall, the chief made his way back to the cave and placed the island's heart back into its rightful place. There was a blinding flash of light before the pulsating glow began again. The chief knew then that everything was going to go back to the way it was before.'

The children clapped and cheered. The other villagers smiled at the children and continued with their tasks. Some children wandered off to play and some stayed back to ask questions.

Is the heart of Tafari really under our island? Asked some.

'Yes, of course the heart is still there, it has stayed there ever since the chief returned it, but you must never take it from its home again or you will all be CURSED!'

Children ran off, screaming in fright.

The tribal elder laughed and hoped those children would remember and pass on the story when they became elders.

Family Day

By Rebekah J.

I jerkily manoeuvre my way around the roundabout with Dad tensely gripping his seat next to mine, the boat tacked onto the back rattling along. The L plates against the windscreen glare at me as I try to change lanes. Windows down because the aircon needs fixing. I see Dad gazing out, boyishly excited for the day to come. It's been a lifetime since we've been out on the water. Traversing through the islands. Too many years for it to surely feel the same.

Pulling into the Marina, I allow Dad to reverse down the ramp, me as the captain shouting from the boat, 'Little to the left ... tad further!' Without warning, a wave of nostalgia washes over me. I remember the days my Mum used to say just that.

* * *

My two older brothers and I were aimlessly waiting on the dock, early morning sun beating down on us while Mum and Dad were doing whatever had to be done. To keep it lively, each would dare the other to walk around the poles tethered to the floating land. With my small hands I covered my face and eyes, squinting with every muscle I had to make the fear of them falling lessen. In my mind, the green cloudy waters beneath screamed of death as I watched one brother after the other, their toes edging around the inch of protruding metal. They laughed and cheered, ignoring their annoying younger sister.

Sulking away, I went to watch the other families as they pottered about preparing for a day they probably wouldn't still remember ten years down the track. Dad pulled our navy boat up beside us while Mum went to go to park the car. I always liked going with her so we could walk back together, and I could natter on just to her alone.

The voyage would take all of twenty minutes after Mum checked to see that we each had sunscreen and hats on. I'd perch up on her lap while watching Dad steer the boat with his feet ever so sturdily on the jumpy water. I think, looking back that he was always at his happiest when steering. Then he was most giving, most tolerant, like nothing could shake the smile off his face. Sheer joy.

I looked to Mum, and she smiled back but quietly, a smile that didn't quite reach her eyes. She was well versed in giving. Her heart was a constant waterfall with all she poured out. But I suppose when the stream dried and cracked, mud was all that lay inside her. A point was reached when she had to stop. And so, with the vessel bumping against the rolling waves tangy with salt, droning on, I nestled into her chest. Sleep came and took me in no time.

The changing vibrations as the motor slackened, drew me up as I swam to the surface from the dark pool of sleep that had enveloped me. I awoke to the exhilarating view of fun. White beaches reflected in Mum's sunnies as the shore drew nearer. Dad had found a perfect hidden spot in a cove along the island. Green trees splashed the background and I could see wonderful coral beneath the boat as I leaned over the side, my fingertips swimming through the ocean. A new world just sitting there for us to soak up and claim the land our own.

I'd sprint ahead once the boat was anchored, sand flicking

behind me while I scoped out the best spot. Blue open skies, blazing rays and lapping water, brightened my memory. Those days, us three would stripe our cheeks yellow with zinc, heave on our reef shoes, tighten our floppy wide brimmed hats and off we'd set. Through the trees that encased the land, where little paths had been cleared by animals, we would trek. Eventually after blisters spawned, we would make our way back down to the rocks against the island itself. My two brothers would scout ahead, so I made friends with the little barnacles, collecting and piling them together into families. The podgy ones that I'd declare parents, would always manage to crawl off without a word. So, naturally, locking up my anger, I would gently place them all back together.

Later wandering slowly, stick in hand and a pocket full of pretty shells, Dad would be waiting for me where the smooth sand meets the course rocks. He never spent much time with Mum alone.

Hours would pass with short swim breaks in between and I swear the holes we dug at those times went all the way to China. Coaxing Mum into one, she was buried alive with nothing but her head and brown threaded hat bobbing above. I'd laugh hysterically and smother her cheeks with kisses. Dad would sit and laugh from his chair but never join in. I watched the distance between them grow larger.

When the afternoon peaked and we were zooming out of the bay on our way home, Dad always made a surprise stop at the abandoned observatory, as if to keep the day going longer. Once our snorkels and flippers were strapped on, we would swim after him while he acted as our own personal fish guide. Dad always had the most interesting things to say.

Mourning the final escapade coming to an end and back in the boat, I'd unstick my goggles that had seared into my raging sunburn. Even though more than thrice throughout the day Mum had lathered me head to toe in greasy sunscreen. With my lips shrivelled like prunes and my hair a pile of seaweed, we all headed back home.

Everyone in the car was quiet—no radio breaking the silence after a day well spent. From the backseat squished between my brothers, I tentatively watched Dad's hand as he fiddled with the broken aircon. When his hand receded, there was a moment of hesitation. Yet he resisted and rested it on the wheel. Mum sat with her legs crossed against the door.

We arrived back home.

Now, standing in the boat alone, I approach this day with weariness and a pathetic scrap of hope. A lifetime has passed. Brothers grown and gone. A new extra house. I've come to accept we never really were the quality time family. But those rare days when we decided to escape the heaviness of home, to leave behind what couldn't be fixed and just pretend we were all in this together exploring the island, have become memories I hold pushed up against my heart, dinting it. I struggle to breath sometimes when these memories resurface. When Mum and Dad could still look at each other with a gleam of love in their eyes. When every room wasn't compressed with tension so tight that even air wouldn't dare to dwell there.

I see Dad walking towards me, and with all I have, I roll in my thoughts, plaster on a smile that reaches my eyes, and hold onto the feeble hope that the island brings back what it's always given, and shout 'Come on, let's go!'

Stolen Innocence

By Jaymie A.

The first signs of morning came, so Loures was left alone to stare at her house. Looming over her, it had never appeared so still. The placidity made her ill. Loures loathed her parents. Her mind was the mind of a preadolescent girl. She wanted to be an artist. She could not help but hold resentment to those who treated her like a child. That's why she had loved spending time with him. He said that he could see what they could not—she was mature for her age.

There was one thing on her mind and pulse as she stood at the gate. The suspense, the unpredictability of the next few moments was agonising. The fear of her parents noticing her absence during the night dawned on her while she was with him. They would be furious. Perhaps exhibiting a fit of hysteria. Loures believed they might not love her after this. However, he had soothed her worries with promises that he would take care of her.

Loures shivered, recalling the warmth of him, which he took as lust, and she mistook for love. The frenzy of mutual obsession might have been eased, if only she was not blinded by innocence. This is what made it so easy for him. Loures was loved plenty at home, although, she had not realised it at the time. This real love, however, came with dissension. It could only be described as infatuation. This is how she thought it was meant to be. Love in books was filled with tenderness and adoration, all the things he gave to her willingly because of his perversion. No matter how romantic she told herself it was, still, she was afraid.

Most nights spent together were filled with soft laughter and conversation that lasted for hours. The last night was different, it felt wrong. The thought of his hands on her body made her skin crawl. Her mind felt conflicted. She thought she was meant to like it, but she felt like she was suffocating. So, as the cloudy haze of her pre-mature idea of romance cleared, she remembered all the times he had held her in ways she did not want. All the times he had said he was the only one she could trust. So, she pushed away her friends and family. The regret sank in fast. The longing of those who were still alive felt like grief in her heart. She wanted nothing but to tell them she had not meant it, that she wanted to be okay again.

She stood there, limp with exhaustion. The same question circled around her mind, whether she would still be welcome at home. Her fingers traced the latch. The gate was the only thing separating her from her home—the ocean between homeland and an isolated island. All she wanted was to cry in her mother's arms and tell her everything that had happened. He had taken things she could never get back. Her innocence, her youth, her trust, everything she once had, now violated.

Loures felt disgusting. She wanted nothing to do with herself. Her skin felt exploited and abused. He had seemed to have loved her so much, she was not sure how he could make her feel this way.

It was possibly the most terrifying thing she could do. The guilt overwhelmed her, telling her parents was the only thing she could do to ease this heartache. She was not sure, however, if her Mum loved her enough to see through what she had done.

Loures pushed herself through the gate. Grass covered in the morning dew brushed under her feet as she walked to the door. Her stomach was in knots telling her to turn back—the tide pulling her back out to sea. Memories of her childhood, only a year ago now, flooded back to her. This very yard, that now seemed like foreign territory, held so many precious memories. The light had once warmed her face, paint brush in her hand, as her Dad had sat beside her helping her with every stroke. Every painting she had created, no matter how terrible she thought they were, he had hung in his room.

Now blurry eyed, Loures fought against the feeling and slowly entered with uncertainty.

Waiting, seated at the table were her parents. Worried looks spread across their faces. They stood up as soon as she entered. Before she had even made it down the hallway, she burst into tears. Overwhelmed with pain she crumpled into her parents' arms. Finally, she was free from the waves of guilt and back safe on stable land. Barely able to compose sentences, Loures sobbed, attempting to explain her absences. Her parents showed their understanding by holding her tighter.

'It was never your fault, my baby.'

A Long Way from Home

By Brooke M.

A life raft was the perfect escape plan for anyone stuck in my situation, a situation of disaster and desperation. My need to survive was strong, but what does one do without a life raft or other survival equipment?

Warm sand finding a place to rest between my toes would be great. The sun resting atop my head, causing a slight tan, would be welcome. My skin would like to glow with serotonin, and light shining from my eyes would fill my soul. However, when all that you desire is forced to the back of your head, it's hard to feel faith and hope in your ability to survive.

Two hundred metres, just two hundred metres separates me from my one chance at making it home. Home to the safety of my Mother's arms, her floral scent filling my nose, calming the flow of my blood.

Sadness, anger, uncertainty race to the forefront of my emotions. The war and peace within my mind, is roaring through the atmosphere, creating so many unanswered questions. Why me? Why am I here? Couldn't the universe have picked someone else, anyone else? Anyone could have fallen off that boat and be left to drown, to sink to the bottom of the ocean. But yet, it's me who found salvation on the small patch of sand, under the one lonely palm tree casting shadows that dance as the sun drifts through the sky.

I sit on the small shore, my bum planted in the sand, my knees bent to my chest. My hands sink into the sand beside me, pushing through the layers to reach the untouched coolness. I draw my hands through the sand, noticing the wet grains under my nails. I bring my feet under me, drawing my body up by using my hands to steady me. My eyes focus above the water, casting around to the many trees and sand dunes only two hundred metres from my feet. The longer I focus my eyes, the further the distance seems, like it is moving away from me, like the ocean is stretching its limbs, stretching the islands farther from one another, their roots no longer connected.

I take a steady step forwards, allowing the tips of my toes to break the surface of the water. The longer I stand motionless, the more the tide steals the sand from under my feet, causing my weight to sway. My hands tighten, drawing into tight fists, gathering all the rage in my body, holding it captive. I allow the feeling to build before releasing the tension, stretching my fingers as far as they will go, feeling each emotion slowly seep from my skin. My body lightens, my head clears. I turn to look at the few metres of sand keeping me hostage. Fallen palm-fronds, light enough to float, enough for my hands to keep them together drift near. I could gather them and tell my legs to give a powerful kick. My path is written, now I just have to follow it.

I gather as many fallen branches as possible, building a pile just inches from the shore. Once I have all the branches within reach, I begin to drag my makeshift raft further into the void I must cross. With each step I take, the water rises closer to my shoulders. Before my head goes under, I use my last step to jump above the water, rising forwards, ensuring to gather my waist and upper body on the raft, allowing my legs to motor me to safety.

The tide draws in and out, the waves ripple along the surface. Using the strength of my arms and legs I continue my journey, the gap slowing closing, the distance become shorter.

I look back the way I came, hope filling my lungs, a yellow glow radiating from my skin. I'm past half-way. I'm going to make it! I'm going to make it home!

As my head turns back to continue my journey, the ocean changes mood. The water begins to swallow each leaf, each branch, slowing pulling my hands with it. I must abort my raft, I must make the rest of the journey by myself, using my own resources, my own strength for survival. I force my weight to my side, sliding away from the wreckage, my eyes focusing ahead, ensuring my head stays above the water. I push my hands through the water, feeling the ocean slice through my fingers, my toes following behind.

My fears cloud my head, the possible outcomes of today waging war circling in my mind. I think of other people, caught in this situation, people who didn't survive the oceans grasp. Those who were drawn to the deepest, darkest parts of the ocean's thoughts, its deepest, scariest secrets. But not me. I will not become a sacrifice of despair. I will survive. I will stay with the sky, the breeze, the roaming of leaves. The endless possibilities of a rainbow. The colours light the sky and the heavens joining us. Showing the light, the way to freedom.

The gap shortens, I can almost touch the dry sand. My lungs become heavy, gasping for air, my arms and legs feel like dead weights, dropping lower and lower through the water. I begin to struggle, the last bit of energy slowing leaving my muscles. I take one last big gasp of air, feeling my lungs expand as much as possible. Taking one last look at the shiny sand, and shade of trees, I lower my head into the water, kicking my legs faster than ever before, the strength of each kick propelling me through the water.

Once I feel my body hook onto the waves, I'm looking forwards again, breathing in the smell of coconuts. My knees scrape the sand below me, feeling sea shells pass my thigh through the water, reminding me of the tide. I crawl the rest of the way, my fingers digging into the sand, picking up fistfuls as I go. With one last shuffle, I reach the dry sand, it consumes me, wraps it warm arms around me, holding me tight. Reviving me from hell. The uneasy sea, all-consuming ready to drag me under.

I collapse onto my right shoulder continuing to roll onto my back, my feet stretched out, still connected to the blue water. I stare up into the sky, hues of blue and fluffs of white flow through the atmosphere. Seagulls sit in the breeze, looking over their home. The ocean and the sky, so similar yet so very different. My hands drop to my side, my palms gathering the light of the sun, filling my body with warmth, happiness and hope.

I draw my shoulders upwards, planting my elbows into the dry sand. I look at my toes as they wiggle, dancing with each other as joy washes through my bones. My eyeline rises to the ocean, to the small island my toes once touched. A smile stretches over my face so wide it almost hurts, and I finally realise, I'm going to make it home.